MW00979387

© 2011 Claudia Rueda
© 2011 Editorial Océano, S.L., Barcelona, Spain
English language translation © 2013 Eerdmans Books for Young Readers

Original Title: Todo es relativo
www.oceano.mx

Published in 2013 by Eerdmans Books for Young Readers,
an imprint of Wm. B. Eerdmans Publishing Co.
2140 Oak Industrial Dr. NE
Grand Rapids, Michigan 49505
P.O. Box 163, Cambridge CB3 9PU U.K.

www.eerdmans.com/youngreaders

Manufactured at Tien Wah Press
in Malaysia in January 2013, first printing

19 18 17 16 15 14 13   9 8 7 6 5 4 3 2 1

Library of Congress Cataloging-in-Publication Data

Rueda, Claudia, author, illustrator.
Is It Big or Is It Little? / by Claudia Rueda; illustrated by Claudia Rueda.
pages cm
Summary: A cat and mouse chase demonstrates such concepts as deep and
shallow, scary and scared, and beginning and end.
ISBN 978-0-8028-5423-0 (alk. paper)
[1. English language — Synonyms and antonyms — Fiction. 2. Cats — Fiction.
3. Mice — Fiction.] I. Title.
PZ7.R885153Eve 2013
[E] — dc23
2012048443

FSC
www.fsc.org
MIX
Paper from
responsible sources
FSC® C012700

Is It Big
or
Is It Little?

Claudia Rueda

Eerdmans Books for Young Readers

Grand Rapids, Michigan • Cambridge, U.K.

Is it big?

or is it little?

Is it deep?

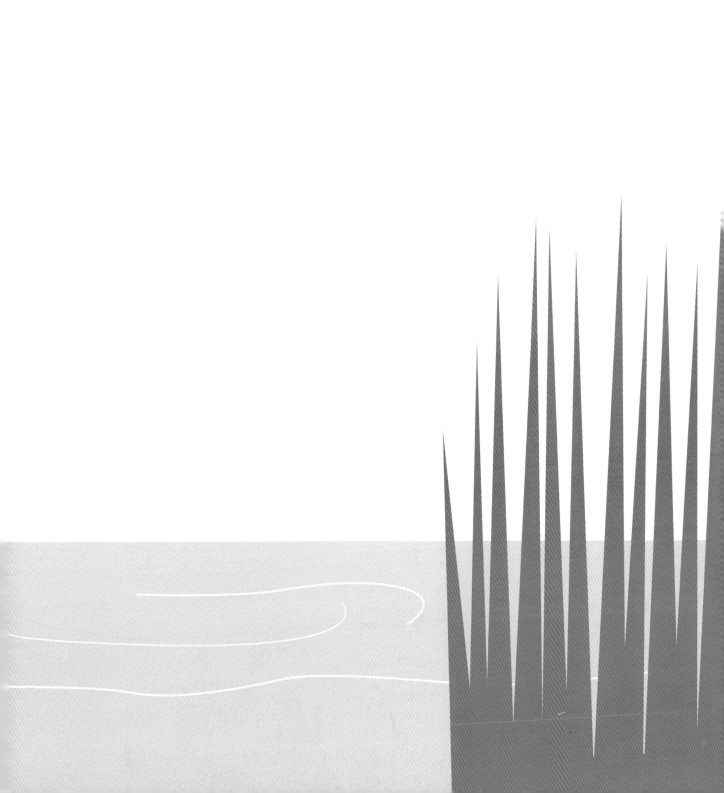

or shallow?

Is it light?

or **heavy**?

Is it long?

or short?

or scared?

Is it the **end** . . .

. . . or is it
the
beginning?